SERGIO

Saves the Game!

by Edel Rodriguez

LITTLE, BROWN AND COMPANY

Books for Young Readers

New York   Boston

Sergio loves soccer.

He kicks

jumps

defends

heads

butts

knees

shoots

. . . and scores!

A true star . . .

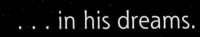

. . . in his dreams.

In the real world, he . . .

trips   falls   crashes

sets   shoots

slips   slides   flips

. . . and scores!   For the other team.

When he plays with his friends,
he's always the last one chosen.

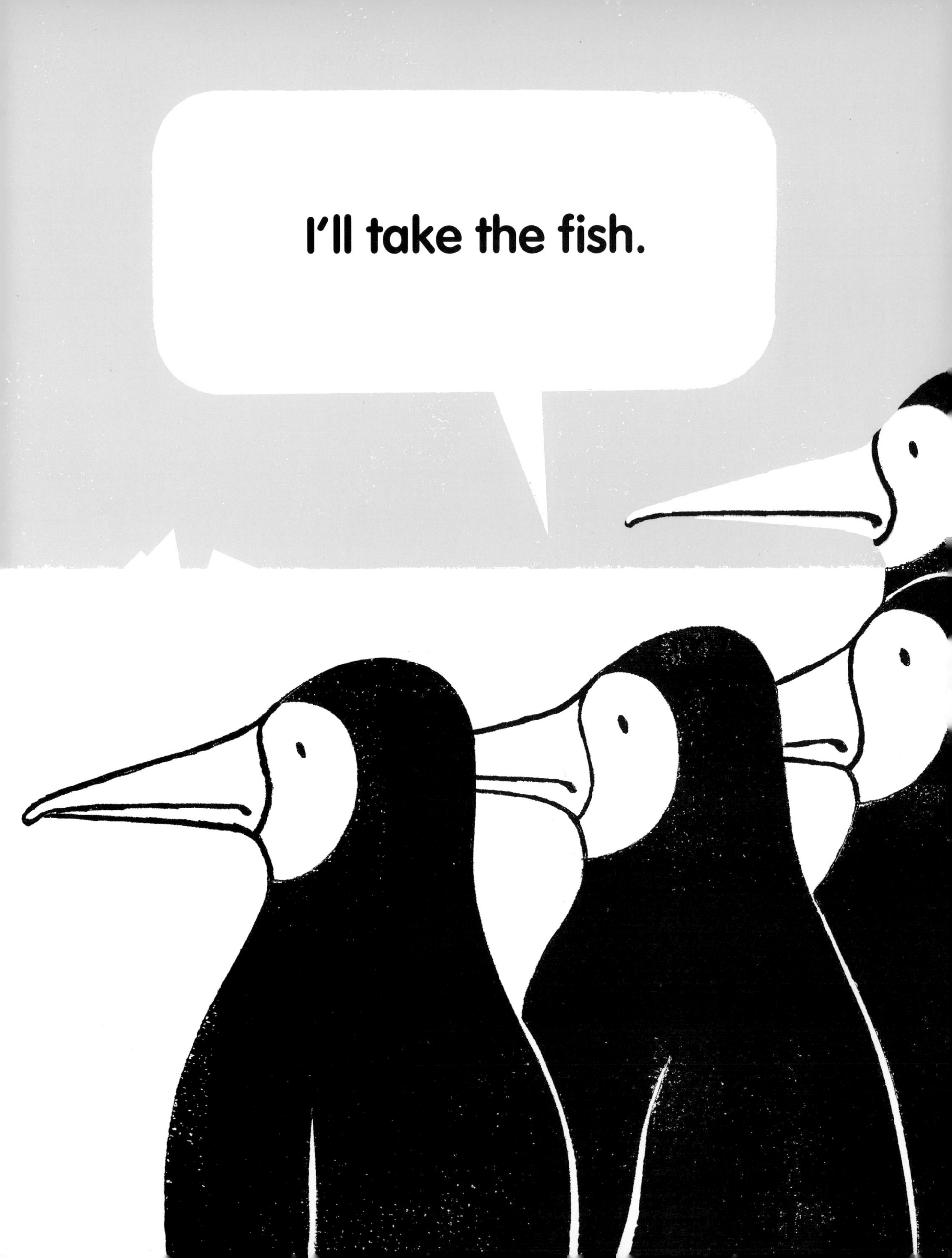
I'll take the fish.

"Mom, no one wants to play soccer with me, I always slip and fall," says Sergio.

"It's not you, it's all this ice!" says his mother. "Why don't you play Ping-Pong instead?"

"But I love soccer," says Sergio.

"Well . . . maybe you can try being the goalie! That's a very important position."

Sergio loves the idea! He hops out the door, and heads out to play . . .

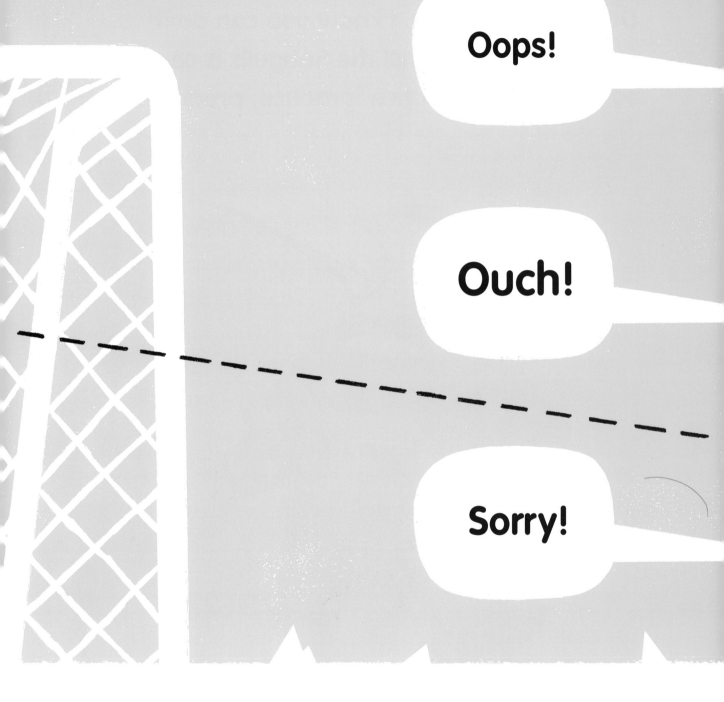

He practices hard for the big game,
but as usual, Sergio has some trouble. . . .

He keeps at it day and night, determined to be ready for the championship. Eventually, Sergio gets pretty good!

The big day arrives and everyone comes out to see who will win the championship—the Penguins or the Seagulls.

The game has its ups . . .

. . . and downs!

The Seagulls are BIG, but Sergio's team is FEISTY! It's not as easy for the Seagulls as they thought it would be.

During the game, Sergio saves one goal after another.

But he loses one when he trips on his shaky tail and the ball bounces right into the net!

It's very hard for the Penguins to get the ball past the Seagulls' large wings.

But they find a way to get one through!

In the end, Sergio's team is winning by one goal, and the Seagulls are down to their final penalty kick.

They send out their biggest player to take the shot. The entire game is now in Sergio's wings!

As the final ball races toward the goal, Sergio remembers everything he has practiced. . . .

Eyes on the ball!
Head down!
Wings up!

"I HAVE TO STOP THIS BALL!"

Well, he stops it, all right!

Sergio's teammates lift him up on their shoulders. They have finally beaten the Seagulls and won the championship!

The entire team celebrates and cheers with joy!

Sergio tries to cheer too, but all he can say is . . .

HMPFMMMPPPPFFFMMMFFFmmmmmfffff!!!

Sergio is finally a true star.

For Jennifer and Sofia

Little, Brown Books for Young Readers

Hachette Book Group
237 Park Avenue, New York, NY 10017
Visit our Web site at www.lb-kids.com

Little, Brown Books for Young Readers is a division of Hachette Book Group, Inc. The Little, Brown name and logo are trademarks of Hachette Book Group, Inc.

First Edition: May 2009

Library of Congress Cataloging-in-Publication Data

Rodriguez, Edel.
    Sergio saves the game / by Edel Rodriguez. — 1st ed.
        p. cm.
    Summary: Although Sergio the penguin loves to play soccer, he is very clumsy and uncoordinated and he practices day and night, hoping he can help his team win the big game against the Seagulls.
    ISBN 978-0-316-06617-4
    [1. Penguins—Fiction. 2. Soccer—Fiction. 3. Clumsiness—Fiction.] I.Title.
PZ7.R618835Sk 2009
[E]—dc22

2008029184

10 9 8 7 6 5 4 3 2 1

SC

Manufactured in China

The illustrations in this book were created with oil-based woodblock ink printed on paper, combined with digital media.